Happy Birthday,
Graham.

Wishing you lots of
ADVENTURES!

Love,
Granny & Grandpa

April 20, 2009

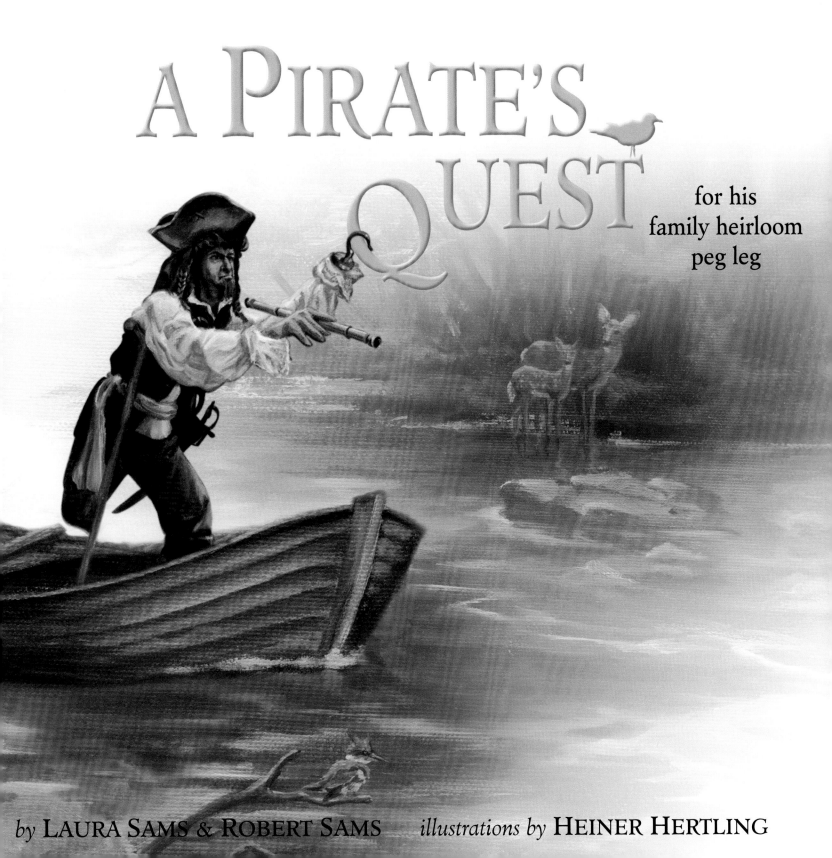

A Pirate's Quest

for his family heirloom peg leg

by LAURA SAMS & ROBERT SAMS illustrations by HEINER HERTLING

Acknowledgements

The authors and illustrator would like to thank Carl R. Sams II and Jean Stoick
for their inspiring photography, support and willingness to take a chance on our story.
We also thank Karen McDiarmid for her artistic contributions,
Greg Dunn for his color expertise, Patti Campbell for her pirate costume design,
Bryce Groark for his underwater photography references, Bruce Montagne (the one-handed pirate),
Jason Weber (the young boy on the beach), Morgan Weber, Christine Sarazin, Becky Ferguson,
Ryan Ferguson, Mark and Deb Halsey, Nancy Higgins, Sandy Higgins and Kirt Manecke.

Special thanks to Diane Hertling, Ron and Diane Sams and the rest of our families
for their suggestions and support over such a long process.
Just as the pirate is dedicated to his family, we are dedicated to you.

This book is based on a song in the educational movie *The Riddle in a Bottle*.
To download *The Family Heirloom Peg Leg Song*,
visit www.apiratesquest.com.

Carl R. Sams II Photography, Inc.

361 Whispering Pines
Milford, MI 48380
800/552-1867   248/685-2422   Fax 248/685-1643
www.apiratesquest.com   www.strangerinthewoods.com   www.carlsams.com

Graphic Design: Karen McDiarmid

A Pirate's Quest: For his family heirloom peg leg
by Laura Sams & Robert Sams, Portland, OR
Illustrated by Heiner Hertling, Milford, MI
Carl R. Sams II Photography, Inc. © 2008

Summary: A one-legged pirate follows moving water on
his quest to find his family heirloom peg leg.

Printed and bound in Canada
Friesens of Altona, Manitoba

ISBN 978-0-9770108-7-5
1. Pirate/Nature/Moving Water–Juvenile fiction.
2. Pirate/Nature/Moving Water–Fiction

Library of Congress Control Number: 2008906378

10 9 8 7 6 5 4 3 2

Dedicated to
those who protect our
rivers, streams, lakes and oceans.

And to those who have lost,
those who have found,
and those who are still searching.

On the shore of a tiny lake
far from the sea,
a one-legged pirate sat and cried.

The peg leg had been in his pirate family
for as long as he could remember.
His one-legged grandpappy had worn it.

His one-legged pappy had worn it.

And he had worn it,
hoping to pass it down
to a one-legged
son or daughter.

He had traveled to this tiny lake to visit
his two-legged sister,
who was famous for her
chocolate pirate ship cookies.

Many pirates claimed they would rather
find a treasure chest filled with her cookies
than a treasure chest
filled with gold.

One evening, the pirate fell asleep
with a belly full
of chocolate ship cookies.

In the morning when he woke,
his peg leg was gone.

"Me peg leg! Me peg leg!"

His family heirloom had fallen into the lake
and drifted away during the night.

The sad, one-legged pirate watched
the water whirling and swirling in the wind,
and an idea began whirling and swirling
in his head.

If the water could carry his peg leg away,
it could carry him too.

The same water that took his leg
could also help him find it.

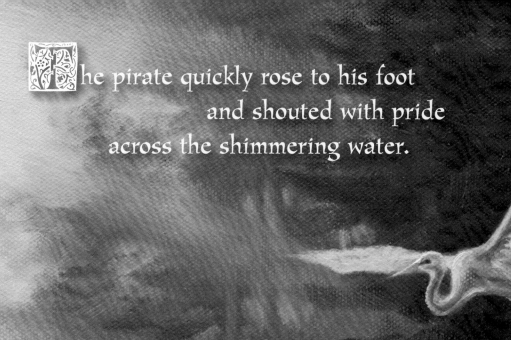

The pirate quickly rose to his foot
and shouted with pride
across the shimmering water.

"I vow that I will never give up.
I'll never stop me quest!
Until I find that beautiful leg,
I promise not to rest!
I know that we shall meet again if I follow the moving water.
And one day I shall pass her on
to me one-legged son or daughter!"

So he searched the lakes,
and followed the streams,

which led to a river . . .

. . . and out to the sea,
where rough and choppy waters
pulled the pirate
farther and farther
from land.

Through his telescope,
the pirate spotted a dark, familiar shape
floating in some yellow seaweed.

"Me peg leg!
Me peg leg!"

He jumped into the waves
and swam as fast as
a one-legged, one-handed pirate
could swim,
until finally he found . . .

. . . a young loggerhead sea turtle.

"Yarrrrr!"

"I vow that I will never give up.
I'll never stop me quest!
Until I find that beautiful leg,
I promise not to rest!"

So he followed the currents,
   which carried him 'round . . .

from island
to island . . .

. . .'til his ship ran aground.

Suddenly, the pirate spotted
a dark, familiar shape
on the reef far below.

"Me peg leg!
Me peg leg!"

He swam down
as fast as a one-legged,
one-handed pirate could swim
until finally he found . . .

. . . the arm of an octopus
who was guarding the entrance to her cave.

"Yarrrrr!"

"I vow that I will never give up.
I'll never stop me quest!
Until I find that beautiful leg,
I promise not to rest!"

So he searched the mangrove forests
growing near the beach,
hoping the tides would carry his leg
back within his reach.

He braved the stormy weather
and even a hurricane,

to see if his leg
would be blown to shore
by gusts of wind and rain.

When the skies were blue again,
    the pirate spotted a dark, familiar shape
        by a jagged rock.

"Me peg leg! Me peg leg!"

He crawled as fast as a one-legged,
one-handed pirate could crawl,
until finally
he found . . .

. . . a wooden peg leg,
    but it already belonged
to another pirate.

The pirate was tired . . .
The pirate was weary . . .
But he pulled himself up
with his last bit of strength.

"Yarrrr!"

"I vow that I will never give up.
I'll never stop me quest!
Until I find that beautiful leg,
I promise not to rest!"

Then he collapsed
and fell asleep
on the sand.

Farther down the beach,
a young boy was searching for hidden treasures
that washed to shore after a long journey at sea.

He picked up an odd piece of driftwood rolling in the surf.

He imagined it looked
like an old peg leg,
which had fallen off a one-legged pirate
on a grand adventure.

As he watched the water
whirling and swirling around him,
an idea began whirling and
swirling in his head.

If the water could carry
a peg leg here,
could it carry a pirate too?
Could that be him?

He quietly slipped the peg leg
onto the pirate's knee.

"There," he whispered.
"It's a perfect fit."

When the pirate woke,
he cried with joy.

"Me peg leg!
Me peg leg!"

He quickly stood tall on
his two legs
and shouted with pride
across the
shimmering water.

"I vowed that I would never give up!
I never stopped me quest!
Until I found me beautiful leg,
I promised not to rest!
I knew that we would meet again if I followed the moving water.
And one day I shall pass her on
to me one-legged son or daughter!"

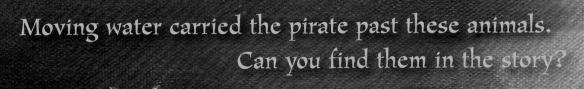

Moving water carried the pirate past these animals.
Can you find them in the story?

Great Horned Owl

Big Brown Bat

Sandhill Cranes

Red Squirrel

FOREST

Great Blue Heron

Black-capped Chickadees

Beaver

Painted Turtle

WETLANDS

Northern Cardinal

White-tailed Deer

Muskrat

Common Loon

Brook Trout

Roseate Spoonbills

Belted Kingfisher

Horseshoe Crab

COASTLI

White Ibis

Green Anole Lizard

Ghost Crab

Moose

Bald Eagle

Laughing Gulls

Brown Pelicans

White Pelican

Great Egret

Humpback Whale

Bottlenose Dolphin

Double-crested Cormorant

OPEN OCEAN

Harbor Seals

Loggerhead Sea Turtle

REEF

Nassau Grouper

Mahi-mahi

Common Atlantic Octopus

Caribbean Reef Shark

"Ahoy mateys!
Do you like music?
Then listen to me peg leg song —
it's what inspired this story.

I'll even let yeh download it for free
on me website,
www.apiratesquest.com."

THE END